The Magic Ringlet

A little girl named Varyusha was given a magic ring by an old soldier. He told her it had powers to bring happiness to her and health to her ailing grandfather. On her way home, the ring slipped off her finger and fell into the deep snow. However much she dug, she couldn't find it. Poor Varyusha! Each day as her grandfather's cough grew worse and worse, she blamed herself for having lost the ring. Then one Spring day when the snows were all melted, Varyusha went to the woods to search for her ring. What she found is the magic of this story.

Printed in U.S.A. All rights reserved. Text © 1971 by Thomas P. Whitney.
Illustrations © 1971 by Leonard Weisgard. Published by Young Scott Books,
a Division of Addison-Wesley Publishing Co., Inc., Reading, Mass. 01867.
Library of Congress Catalog Card No. 71-155911. SBN: 201-09277-8.

9277

The
MAGIC
RINGLET

BY
**Konstantin
Paustovsky**

TRANSLATED BY
Thomas P. Whitney

ILLUSTRATED BY
Leonard Weisgard

YOUNG SCOTT BOOKS

Grandfather Kuzma lived with his granddaughter Varyusha in the tiny village of Mokhovoye, a name which in Russian means "mossy," at the edge of the forest.

Right in the middle of the winter, Grandfather Kuzma ran out of *makhorka*—a strong, coarse, pungent Russian kind of tobacco. He began to cough badly. He complained of weakness. And he kept saying that if he could just have a puff or two of makhorka, he would surely feel better right off.

And so Varyusha set out that same Sunday to the
neighboring and larger village of Perebory to get some
makhorka for her grandfather.

Perebory had a railroad running through it. After Varyusha bought the makhorka, she went over to the station to watch the trains go by.

Two soldiers were sitting on the station platform. One had a beard and jolly gray eyes.

The locomotive was roaring in from afar. And Varyusha could already see it emerging from the distant, dark forest and hurtling toward them, wreathed in its steam.

"It's the express!" exclaimed the soldier with the beard. "Watch out there, little girl. The train will blow you right away."

The steam engine fairly flew at the station. Snow blew up into their eyes. And the big wheels whirled, clicking and clacking along the rails as if they were chasing one another down the track. Varyusha grabbed a light pole and shut her eyes tight—just as if she were really afraid of being lifted up over the ground and dragged along behind the train.

When the train had passed, the bearded soldier asked Varyusha, "What have you got there in the little bag?"

"Makhorka," she replied.

"Will you sell it to me? I need a smoke badly."

"Grandfather Kuzma wouldn't want me to," Varyusha replied primly. "It's for his cough."

"Well, just listen to that!" said the soldier. "Mighty strict you are for such a little flower wearing felt boots!"

"Well, you can take what you need, anyway." Varyusha held out the bag to the soldier.

The soldier poured a good-sized fistful of the makhorka into his overcoat pocket, then rolled up a paper funnel like a tiny pipe and put some makhorka in, and lit it up. He chucked Varyusha beneath the chin and looked merrily into her blue eyes.

"My goodness!" he declared. "Now what can I give you in return?"

He took from his pocket a little steel ring, blew the makhorka shreds off it, wiped it on his coat sleeve, and popped it onto Varyusha's middle finger.

"This ringlet is magic. Wear it as long as you choose."

"And just what is it that makes it magic?" asked Varyusha, blushing.

"Because," explained the soldier, "if you wear it on your middle finger, it will bring you health, both you and your grandfather. And if you put it on this fourth finger here, then you're going to have a great big enormous happiness. Or, if you want to go forth and see the whole wide world with all its wonders, just put the ringlet on your index finger, and it will never fail you!"

"Oh, thank you!" said Varyusha. And she ran off toward her home in Mokhovoye.

A wind blew up and a thick, thick snow was falling. Varyusha kept touching the ringlet on her finger, turning it about, looking at it, admiring its gleam in the winter light.

"Now why did the soldier forget to tell me what would happen if I put it on my little finger?" she thought to herself. "What will happen if I do? I think I will just try it and see what happens."

She put the ringlet on her little finger. The finger was tiny, tiny. And the ringlet would not stay on it at all. Suddenly, it slipped off and fell into the deep snow near the trail.

Varyusha cried out and started to dig down into the snow with her hands. She dug and dug but she could not find the ringlet. Her fingers soon became blue from the cold snow. They got stiff and wouldn't bend.

She began to cry. The ringlet had been lost. Grandfather Kuzma would not regain his health. She would never have that great big enormous happiness. And she would not see the whole wide world with all its wonders.

Varyusha stuck an old pine branch in the snow to mark the spot where she had dropped the ringlet, and she went on home. She wiped her tears away with her mitten, but they kept on coming all the same and they froze on her face.

Grandfather Kuzma was delighted to get his makhorka, and with it he smoked up the whole cabin. He listened to Varyusha's story about the ringlet and said, "Don't grieve, little one. The ringlet is still right there where you dropped it. Why don't you ask Sidor about it? He will help you find it."

The old sparrow, Sidor, was sleeping on a stick, puffed up into a ball to keep warm. Sidor lived in Grandfather Kuzma's cabin and was mighty independent about it too, acting as if he owned it.

The very next day, Varyusha caught Sidor, wrapped him up in a kerchief, and took him into the woods. Only the very tip end of the pine branch she had left there was still sticking out of the snow. Varyusha put Sidor on its tip and told him, "Dig about a bit! Find it for me!"

But Sidor merely cocked his head, looked down dubiously at the snow, and cheeped back, "Look here! Look here! I'm no such fool! Look here! Look here!"

He repeated this over and over again and then leapt from the branch into the air and flew back to the cabin.

And so the ringlet was not found.

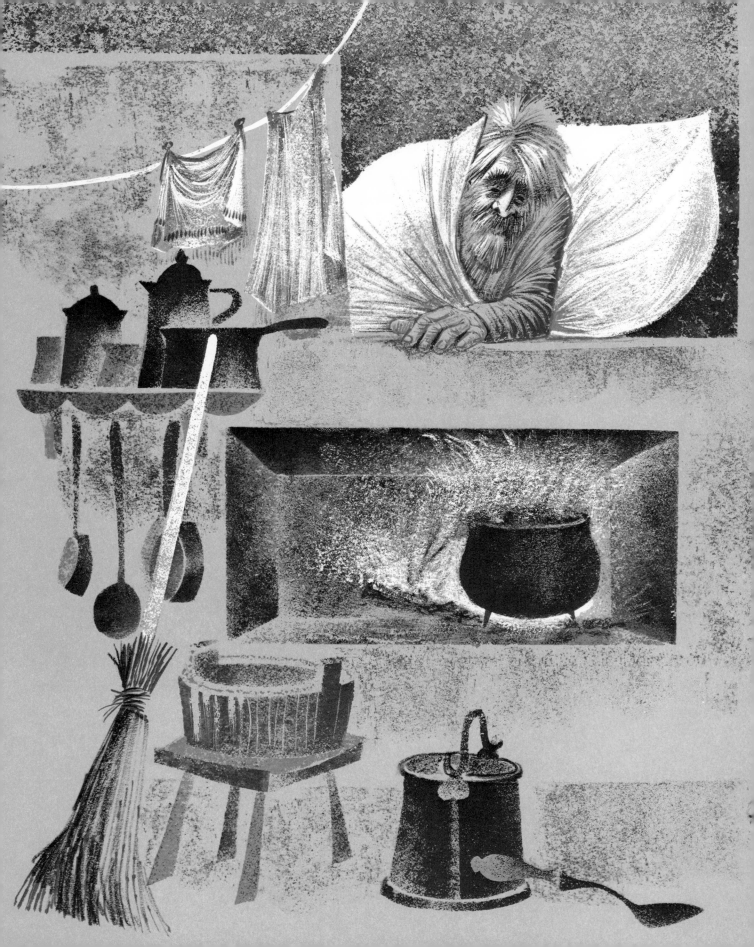

Grandfather Kuzma's cough kept getting worse and worse. As spring drew near he climbed up on top of the big Russian stove. He hardly ever came down from it and kept asking more and more often for something to drink. And Varyusha would give him cold water in an iron dipper.

The snowstorms whirled over the tiny village and buried the cabins. The pines were deep in snow, and Varyusha no longer could find the place in the woods where she had dropped the ringlet.

Often, hidden away behind the big stove, she would weep quietly, feeling sorry for her grandfather and scolding herself. "Stupid! You fooled around and you dropped the ringlet. That's what you get for that!" And she would beat herself on her forehead with her little fist, punishing herself.

Then Grandfather Kuzma would ask her, "What are you making so much noise about?"

"It's Sidor," she would reply. "He has become so naughty and keeps trying to stir up a fight."

One morning Varyusha awakened to find Sidor jumping at the window, pecking away at the glass. She opened her eyes and blinked. Long drops were dripping from the roof in swift pursuit of one another. A warm light poured in through the window. Outside, the jackdaws were making a big racket.

Varyusha opened the door and peered out. A warm wind blew into her eyes and rumpled her hair. "Spring has come!" she said.

The black branches glistened. The wet snow swished as it slipped down off the roof. The damp forest rustled proudly and gaily out there on the village outskirts.

It was spring sweeping through the fields and woods like a young housewife sweeping her way through the house.

Each day the surface of the snow in the woods grew darker and darker. On it appeared, first of all, the brown pine bark which had fallen upon it during the course of the winter. And then, soon after, a multitude of branches appeared where the storms of December had broken them off the trees.

And then through the snow gleamed the yellow of the fallen leaves of the past autumn. Where the snow had completely disappeared, bare patches of ground grew bigger and bigger. And at the edges of the last drifts of all to melt, there bloomed the first flowers, the snakeroot.

One day Varyusha went out to the woods and found the old pine branch which she had stuck in the snow. She began to scrape about very carefully among the old leaves and the empty cones dropped there by the woodpeckers, among the twigs and the rotting moss. And suddenly she saw something gleaming from beneath a black leaf. Varyusha exclaimed with joy. There was the steel ringlet! And it hadn't rusted the least little bit.

Varyusha picked it up, put it on her middle finger, and ran home.

As she was running, she saw Grandfather Kuzma come out of the hut and sit down on top of a pile of earth which lined the outside of the cabin to insulate it from the winter cold. And from him, the blue makhorka smoke rose straight up to the sky, making it seem as if Grandfather was drying out in the spring sun and steam was rising from him.

"Well, well," said Grandfather to Varyusha. "You little rascal, you ran out of the house so quickly you forgot to shut the door behind you, and the whole cabin filled up with spring air. And my illness left me right away. So now I am having myself a smoke. Then I shall take my axe and cut some wood so we can fire up the oven and bake some rye cookies."

Varyusha laughed and said, "Oh, thank you, my ringlet! You see, Grandfather Kuzma, it did make you well!"

Varyusha wore the ringlet the whole day long on her middle finger to drive away her grandfather's illness once and for all. And only in the evening, when she lay down to sleep, did she take the ringlet off her middle finger and put it on her fourth finger. For this was to bring her a great big enormous happiness. However, it was slow to come, and Varyusha went off to sleep before it arrived.

The next morning, she got up early, dressed herself, and went out of the cabin. A quiet dawn had settled over the earth. The stars were still burning brightly at the very edge of the heavens. Varyusha could hear something gently ringing in the forest.

She bent her head and listened hard. White snowdrops were shaking their heads, nodding to the dawn, and each tiny bell-like blossom was lightly jingling, as if a small bug, acting as a bell-ringer, were inside.

And right at that very moment, high up in a tree, gleaming brightly in the golden light of the early morning, an oriole sang out.

Varyusha laughed loudly and her voice echoed and reechoed through the woods. She ran home. And the great big enormous happiness—so big you could not hold it in both your hands—rang and sang in her heart.

Varyusha thought now about putting the ringlet on her index finger so she could see the whole world with all its marvels, but she looked at the flowers, at the sticky little birch leaves, at the clear sky, and she listened to the roosters crowing back and forth, and to the gurgling of the water, and to the whistling of the birds in the fields, and she decided not to put the ringlet on her index finger after all.

"There's no hurry," she said to herself. "There is no place on earth so lovely as Mokhovoye. Grandfather Kuzma was right when he said our own land is a real heaven and that there is no place so good in the whole wide world."

About the Author

Konstantin Paustovsky was born in Moscow in 1892, the son of a railway statistician. Though he wrote in Russian and lived most of his life in Moscow, Paustovsky was more Ukrainian Cossack than Russian. After attending Kiev University, he entered writing via journalism, working as a newsman for more than a decade. His first published work appeared before the revolution, but he did not really make his mark as a professional writer until publication of his successful novel, *Kara-Bogaz*.

From then on Paustovsky wrote prolifically. His subjects ranged widely, through the favorite and typical Russian subjects of nature, remote Soviet areas, famous Russian literary personalities, and sea stories. But his best work was his marathon autobiography entitled *The Story of a Life*. In this sensitive account of his life and times, Paustovsky bridges the chasm between the old and the new Russia. In the years from Stalin's death in 1953 until his own death in 1968, he was a leader in the struggle for greater freedom of creative self-expression in the Soviet Union.

In addition to his longer works Paustovsky wrote some delicate and lovely short stories—and one of the most beautiful of these is *The Magic Ringlet*.

THOMAS P. WHITNEY